The Immortal Cure (Paranormal)

Morgan Reeves

Copyright © 2024 by Morgan Reeves

All rights reserved.

No portion of this book may be reproduced in any form without written permission from the publisher or author, except as permitted by U.S. copyright law.

Contents

1. Chapter One — 1
2. Chapter Two — 10
3. Chapter Three — 17
4. Chapter Four — 28
5. Chapter Five — 42
6. Chapter Six — 50
7. Chapter Seven — 56
8. Chapter Eight — 64
9. Chapter Nine — 70
10. Chapter Ten — 79
11. Chapter Eleven — 88
12. Chapter Twelve — 94
13. Chapter Thirteen — 104
14. Chapter Fourteen — 115
15. Chapter Fifteen — 129

Chapter One

Life as I knew it had pretty much been like a roller coaster. I had been attacked by a Vampire, ensuing a war. Soon followed by befriending some, and beginning a romantic relationship with one. It was a very strange life, and I sure hadn't expected any of it.

Thankfully, since the last time I'd near died, things had settled down. Everything had smoothed out, and no one had yet tried to take my life again. Dodge was indeed still out there somewhere, and sooner or later he would find out that I had not died, and the chase would once again be on.

I was finally in my last year of school, and looked forward to the end of it. I was looking forward to beginning my adult life. I wasn't sure as to what I was going to be doing afterwards, but to me, it didn't really matter, I had what mattered to me the most, and the rest would eventually sort itself out.

In order to maintain some form of normalcy, I had attained myself an easy job at a local restaurant. I hadn't been there long, but I enjoyed it, however, Duke was constantly on my tail about not needing to be there. He was a wealthy man, so was his family, therefore there was no need for me to be wasting my time. I disagreed.

"Hey Malory" I greeted as I walked into work after school Monday morning.

"Hey sweetie" She smiled as she stood at the counter, serving a couple waiting hand in hand.

Malory was a coworker of mine. She was a few years older than me, her hair a short bob brown, roughly tied up into a ponytail. Her eyes were a light blue, contrasting her pale featured face.

I made my way into the back of the restaurant where my apron was kept. I began tying it around my my waist when I noticed a familiar face come into view

"Afternoon Rosie" It was the Irish tinged voice of Callum Connor

"Afternoon" I called back with a wave of my hand

Callum was the cook. He was a year older than me and had been working at the restaurant for about 3 years. He was about six foot, lanky but firm, in some way, his figure was similar to Duke's. Callum was charming and extremely charismatic, and since day one, I had always felt comfortably drawn to him. It was as if I had known him for years, freely talking with him about anything. Except for, of course, my new found fictional family.

"How was school?" He asked as I absorbed in the beautiful sound of his accent

"Same as always I guess, couldn't wait to get out of there" I shrugged, rolling my green workshirt sleeves up to my elbows

He gave a laugh and continued chopping meat vigorously into tiny pieces. Callum was a very attractive man, and when I had discovered he was single, I was shocked. I couldn't understand why he never had dates or girls hanging around outside waiting for him likes flies in summer. He had told me that he wasn't looking for a relationship, and that he had other priorities. I had always wondered what they were, but had never asked him.

I took a hold of my small notebook and pen and began around the unique popular venue.

It was a large restaurant, unlike the restaurant I had first worked for with Clora. My shifts were mostly, Thursdays, Fridays and weekends, usually when the place was filled up to its knees in customers. Thursdays were the roughest, alcohol was cheaper and many teenage boys would overindulge, almost always resulting in one hitting on me. Thankfully, it was a lot easier with Callum around, he would always swoop in and save me when I struggled to save myself.

Once I had served my customers, I handed Callum their orders and leaned over the front counter where Malory was running over the book of reservations.

"What are you doing after work?" She asked me as she leaned her face on a hand

"Nothing" I shrugged. I would be going back home to Duke, Riley and Jaymi.

"Come to the movies with me?" She asked, standing up straight

"What movie? What time?" I asked as I retied my long hair into a high ponytail.

She shrugged again "Any, and as soon as we both finish work"

I gave her an unsure look, tilting my head sideways

She rolled her eyes "I just couldn't be bothered going home to Laz. He's been under so much stress lately because of this whole business screw up, so he's always cranky" She explained, as I smiled at her sympathetically.

Laz was her boyfriend, he was a lawyer and had recently lost a very personal case.

"Sure" I agreed, all too willing to cheer her up

"Cool" She spoke, seeming a little more enthusiastic this time.

I made my way back over to Callum behind the kitchen just as he dinged a meal ready.

"You and Mal going out afterwards?" He asked as I took a hold of two chicken and salad filled plates. I walked towards the young couple seated not too far away, handing them their meals before returning to Callum.

"Yeah, Laz is still freaking out about that case, so she wants to keep distance until it cools off" I answered Callum

"Where are you going?" He asked as he sliced effortlessly into tomatoes and onions

"Movies"

"When?" He continued

"Whenever we both finish" I shrugged

"Well, I'm inviting myself, I'll tag along too" He smirked smug

I rolled my eyes, expecting it. He had a habit of inviting himself out with us, or magically showing up out of nowhere when Malory or I were out. I didn't complain, he was good company.

As the night progressed, Malory remained in her bored position, only faking a smiley happy mood when customers would stroll in.

Callum and I would casually chat when we found the time. If I had spare time, I enjoyed filling it with learning my ways around the cooking department of the restaurant.

"So, how are you and Duke?" Callum asked as he locked up for the night, Malory and myself waiting. It was closing time, exactly eleven o'clock.

"Good" I leaned on the kitchen wall, watching him. Malory and Callum knew Duke existed, but that was as far as details went. I found myself careful when it came to talking about my mythical boyfriend with Callum. Duke had picked me up from work on one occasion, and I just happened to be standing with Callum, deep in conversation. Instantly I knew they disliked each other. I wasn't sure exactly why, but I assumed it had been typically the threat of attention and domination. Duke seemed to worry more about Callum than the other way around, which I had should of expected.

Duke had expressed on numerous occasions that there was something about him he didn't like. I put it down to paranoia.

Malory has easily taken to him of course, what female didn't when they'd met him?

"What time is he expecting you home?" Callum continued as Malory sighed behind me in a gesture for Callum to hurry up

"Whenever" I watched as he locked the final front doors.

Callum and I took my car, Malory in her own as we drove two blocks left where the movie theatre was.

"There's something strange about your boyfriend Rosie" Callum began while we were stopped at a red light

I rolled my eyes "He's a little different than most, but he's a great man, sweet, charming, kind" I defended

He shook his head "Different all right" He agreed, implying something else

"Why does it bother you so much?" I asked, the light ahead turning green

He shrugged "Because you're my friend Rosie, and I care about you. Something about him just doesn't sit well with me, that's all"

"One day I hope you decide to think otherwise of him" I sighed

He rolled down his window, the wind ruffling around his caramel colored hair.

"And what about school, how are your grades?" He asked. If only he understood how alike he and Duke really were.

I gave him a small smile as I followed Malory's dark blue BMW into the parking lot.

"Sorry" He apologised as I parked my car beside's Malory

"My grades are perfectly fine anyway just for your information" I answered as we hoped out of our cars.

Chapter Two

I was about three hours late for school, but I had made it. I didn't want to miss out on anymore classes, I couldn't afford to.

The day went by fast, despite it being tiring and repetitive. On days as such, I wanted to throw my hands up and quit, surrendering to Dukes requests, but had to do what I had to do. In the end, it would be worth it.

During my free period, I studied, exactly like I should have. Luckily it was helping, I needed all the time I could get.

When school did finish, I drove towards work, just to drop in and say hello to Callum and Malory before heading back home.

"Hey you, it's your day off why are you even here?" Callum asked as soon as he spotted me behind the kitchen counter

"Thought I'd drop in and say hi" I shrugged as I walked towards the counter where Malory was.

"Hey" She greeted as she smiled at me, a little happier than usual this time

"How was your day?" I asked her, leaning my elbows on the counter as she scribbled down reservations in the book for Thursday night

"Not bad" She shrugged "Although I'm getting tired of listening to Callum whinge that you aren't working today, no offence" She scoffed

I creased my eyebrows and looked her "What was he saying about me?" I asked curiously

She shrugged again "Same as always, he's worried about you, worried about your boyfriend" She explained leaning down

"Why?" I asked, rolling my eyes

"I think he has a mild crush on you, he wants you to dump Duke so he can have you" She smiled with a wink

"Are you serious?" My mouth gapped

"I am one hundred percent serious, but if you'd prefer me to lie to you, I can" She smiled, wagging her eyebrows up and down

I groaned, turning towards the kitchen, walking towards Callum.

I had tried to ignore the fact, but it was now becoming obvious to others, it made me feel uneasy. Not because I had a boyfriend, but because whenever Callum was around, I felt an unexplainable connection to him, a draw to his normalcy. I dreaded the idea of his feelings being reciprocal from me.

"Hey Callum" I began, keeping my voice steady. He was behind his bench, peeling potatoes when his eyes lifted to me.

"I should tell you to go home on your day off, but to be honest, I like your company" He started, already pulling the charm

I rolled my eyes, and crossed my arms "Callum.." I began

"I know, I'm being too forthcoming, I shouldn't, I'm sorry" He sighed, his eyes kept down on his job in hand

I paused, unsure as to the authenticity of his admittance.

"It's a quiet night" I quickly changed the subject

"Yeah, hopefully I can leave early" He nodded, a small smile forming on his lips as he bravely looked up at me. I had to control my thoughts, the small smiles that he sent my way were sending my heart on a flutter. Not as intense as Dukes eye contact would, but still enough to make me self conscious.

"Well, I'm working tomorrow, so I'll see you then" I finished, cutting into the settling silence, turning to leave

"Okay, drive safe" He waved me off.

I walked outside into the cold winter breeze towards my car. Jumping into the drivers seat, I made sure to check my phone, pulling it from my handbag. There were no missed calls or texts.

I turned the key into the ignition, twisting it to start, but to my confusion, it began to made a conking noise, spluttering angrily before it died back into silence. I tried again, twice, only availing to the same outcome.

I slammed my fists down on my steering wheel cursing. Sitting motionless, I attempted to decide the next course of action. Minutes later, I pulled my phone back out and dialled Duke's number.

He picked up on the second ring, his voice thick with worry.

"My car won't start" I sighed, trying to keep my anger calm

"Where are you?" He asked as I cringed.

He knew I wasn't rostered on for the day, and I knew that my being here, would cause an argument.

"Work" I grit my teeth

"Work?" He repeated

"I wanted to see how Malory was doing after last night" I half lied, trying to ease the situation

"I'll be there soon" He grumbled before hanging up on me

"Love you too Duke" I scoffed as I slammed my phone down in the middle console

I sat there for a moment and tapped my foot impatiently on the floor. Duke was going to make a big deal, after all, it was meant to be my afternoon with him, not at work, no matter how short the stay. He hated that I worked, he hated Callum. I knew I was in for it.

I got out of the car, closing the door shut behind me, just as I did, a gush of wind ran through me. Duke was now standing directly in front of me, his hands by his sides as he took a quick up and down glance at me.

I'd become accustomed to the up and down glances. He was forever making sure I wasn't hurt. It was a paranoia of his, but a logical one that reassured me it was only because he cared.

Swiftly, he moved towards the front of my car pulling the hood up with ease.I moved beside him, watching what he was, watching what his hands were doing, searching for that something missing, broken or out of place.

The minutes passed, his face was unreadable, just as confused as my own

Moving my gaze from his hands, I realised his expression had changed, drastically. He appeared concerned, angry, his eyebrows pulled together in the middle.

Slowly, I glanced between his face back to his fingers. His touch remained frozen inside the engine bag. It was when he lifted three cables that I understood his anger. The cables had clearly been cut from their correct placement.

I lifted my hand, lightly tracing over them in disbelief.

"Someone cut them?" I mumbled "But I was only inside for five minutes, less" I looked back up towards Duke.

Chapter Three

"School holidays are in a week" I mumbled while I lay on Dukes chest in his room

"Does that mean I'll have you all to myself for four weeks?" Duke asked his hand stroked my hair

I shrugged "Depends on how much I work"

He sighed "Hopefully not that much"

"Hopefully" I agreed. It would be nice to spend my time with Duke alone for the four weeks I would be school free.

"I'm still concerned about my car" I mumbled, thinking out loud

"You shouldn't be. We're going to be keeping an eye on it" Duke replied

"If you're worried about it, then I am too"

"You have other things to worry about Rosie. Like school, like your grades.." He trailed off

"But none of that matters if I'm going to be dead"

"Don't think that way, I don't like it" He gave me a small squeeze

"It's nearly happened before" I shrugged

"Nearly. But I have and will always been there to stop it, no matter what" He continued

I sighed and inhaled Duke's sweet scent, letting it fill me up.

"You should take this time to catch up on sleep" Duke mumbled as he leaned down to kiss my forehead

I snuggled closer and mentally agreed. I needed the sleep, especially if I wanted Duke to wake me up on time tomorrow morning for school.

The next morning, Duke woke me up at six in the morning. I readied myself for school and for once, left on perfect time.

"Morning" Clora greeted as she skipped up next to me, Kenai close in tail as he slung an arm around my shoulder.

"Afternoon" I joked back as we made our way to first class.

It was hard to focus on school and work when there were so many things running through my head. I would think of Duke and how close we had become. I would think of Callum and the so called danger that hung around his existence. I also thought about the cables in my car, and who could have possibly been to blame.

By the end of the day, Duke had messaged me, informing me that my car was fixed and waiting for me in the student parking lot. I was relieved, and walked towards it with Clora when the final bell had sounded.

"Are you working this afternoon?" She asked as we got into my car

"Yes, but not for another hour" I shrugged as I backed up out of the parking lot.

"Lets go to Delrose Cafe for hot chocolate" She suggested with a smile.

I drove towards the Cafe across from school and parked my car just outside of the window that we chose to sit in front of. I didn't want my car to be out of view, just in case the cable cutter was to show up again.

"How is work going by the way? I hear Callum has been all over you" Clora began as we sat in our booth, catching up on gossip

"How do you know that?" I asked, my eyebrows creasing together as a tall lanky waitress sauntered over towards us.

She shrugged "Malory told me"

"What can I get you guys today?" The waitress asked as she stood above our booth, holding a notepad and pen in front of herself. She looked bored, probably just wanting to go home to be with her significant other or bed.

"White hot chocolate for me" I gave her small sympathetic smile as if to say 'I know how you feel'.

"I'll get a cappuccino" Clora ordered as she clasped her hands together in front of herself

"Coming up" The waitress smiled, the gesture still not reaching her eyes as she walked off

"So how come you don't ask him on a date?" Clora wondered

"Who?" I asked, playing stupid as I shuffled my eyes around the red themed cafe

"Don't play stupid with me" She sighed as she tilted her head sideways

I shrugged "I have a boyfriend"

She gave me another ridiculous look "Oh, yeah, that boyfriend that I only ever met once. The one that looks like he is going to kill everyone that goes near you. I mean, he's gorgeous and that, but Callum is so your type, I mean, he's exactly your type, and he's Irish" Clora continued dreamily

"Why don't you ask him out Clora?" I asked, flipping it on her.

Clora and the boyfriend she'd last had hadn't exactly worked out, not after he was caught making out with another girl at school. I didn't expect it, and neither did she. She had been heartbroken and it had taken months for her heart to mend.

"Cause I like them bad and rebellious" Clora winked as the waitress returned with our beverages in hand

"Here you are" She spoke, placing our drinks in front of us as we thanked her

I held my mug up to my mouth and blew on the steam.

"I'm not going to let this go Rosalie" Clora eyed me off.

I chose to ignore her.

"What are you doing after work?" Clora gave in when she realised boy talk was over.

"Going home" I answered simply

"Why don't you invite Callum and Malory out with us. We can go ice skating or something" She shrugged as she picked up her cup mimicking what I was doing

"It'll be too late"

"What time do you finish? And don't even lie to me, I have Malory's phone number, I'll just ring and ask" She pointed a finger at me.

"We close at eight tonight" I admitted truthfully

"Meet you guys at the rink at eight thirty then" Clora smiled proudly

"Fine" I gave in, taking a mental note to ensure I told Duke of my plans

"What are you doing during the holidays?" I asked my friend through breaths over my beverage

"Not sure yet, hopefully my parents will take me somewhere exotic and warm" She shrugged as she stared into space, dreaming of it

"That would be good" I dreamed off with her

The rest of our chatting consisted of school, holidays and her worries of failing english. I had similar worries, but it was a lot more intense than just failing english.

After 40 minutes, we made our way back to my car where I drove to Clora's house to drop her off. Once done, I made my way to work.

"Hey Rosie" Malory happily greeted when I walked in

"Afternoon" I smiled in return, sensing her unusually good mood

"You're in a good mood today" I noted as I walked up to the counter

"I am. Laz has been doing better" She admitted

"That's great news Malory" I told her, genuinely happy for her

She just nodded and smiled as she chewed her bottom lip, almost as if in a daze. I wondered suddenly how much make up sex had created her euphoric daydream.

I laughed to myself and walked towards the back of the restaurant where Callum was humming, bobbing his head to the music that beamed from a small old radio nearby.

"Hey" He greeted as soon as I rounded the corner

"Hey there" I greeted back casually.

I walked to the back of the resaurant and changed into my work uniform before returning to where Callum was. There was, as always, only a few customers, already taken care of as another waitress, Faith took their orders. She was fifteen and came from a pretty bad home life. She loved being at work, it gave her financial independence, and an excuse to get out of the house. I admired her courage.

I sighed, looking around as I tied my apron around my waist.

"Something up?" Callum asked as he still bobbed his head to the music playing

I strolled over towards him "What are you doing after work?"

"Depends on what your offer is" He smiled a devilish grin.

"Ice skating. Clora wants us all to all go together"

He nodded amongst his bobbing head "Sounds good"

I began to walk out from the kitchen when Callums voice stopped me.

"Hey, I was wondering, how did you get home last night?" He asked, taking me by surprise

"Duke. Why?"

"What was wrong with your car?" He asked, obviously seeing it as he had left work

"Oh" I started "Some hoodlums cut my cables. It wouldn't start" I shrugged casually. He stopped what he was cutting and stared at me without blinking

"Someone cut your cables?" He repeated

I nodded "Probably just some prank"

"That's a pretty serious prank Rosie" He continued, looking equally as worried as Duke had when he'd discovered it.

I shrugged again walking out from the kitchen, beginning to take my orders. I had hoped that it would have been the end of it, but unfortunately for me, it wasn't.

"Did you report it?" Callum continued as I returned to hand him ordered meals

"No"

"You should have"

"What's the point, what can they do to find the culprit?" I asked, tilting my head at him

He didn't say anything, just gave me a look that spelt defeat.

"So is your boyfriend alright with you coming out with us tonight?" He dared ask.

Chapter Four

"What happened to your hands?" Duke asked, his arms over his chest when I arrived home

He was calm, thankfully.

"I tripped at ice skating" I lightly joked as I held my bandaged hands up

To my surprise, his lips lightly turned up, his arms wrapping around my waist, pulling me close

"Always hurting yourself aren't you?" He breathed as he walked me into the living room.

I shrugged and leaned into him, soaking in his scent

"No matter what I do, I just can't seem to help it" I mumbled against his thin shirt

He rest a hand on the back of my head, the other on the small of my back. I lifted my face and looked up at him, his eyes were searching my face

"You're in an unusually good mood" I smirked

He shrugged and leaned down, his hand reaching out to my face.His thumb began rubbing circles around my cheek"I trust you, at the end of the day, you come home to me" He explained

"That's right" I smiled as he leaned down to lightly press his lips against mine

"Can I ask you something?" I began

"What is it?" He mumbled as he fiddled with a piece of stray hair near my forehead

"Can you be honest?"

"Sure" He answered, now looking at me directly, curious

"What do you know about Callum that I don't?" I edged

He sighed and dropped his hand from my face "I don't want to talk about him" He weakly smiled, leaning down to kiss me again, this time, gentle, slow, passionate

I didn't argue, I didn't press the issue. I supposed that tomorrow night, all would be revealed when Callum spoke to me after work.

"Where is everyone?" I asked, looking around the house

"Heya" Riley's voiced entered on time as he walked downstairs, stopping at the bottom.

"Riley! Hey!" I grinned

"You're up super late tonight. Ditching school tomorrow are we?" He asked, winking at me

"No" I rolled my eyes

"Sure sure" He mumbled as he walked towards us, stopping a few feet away

"Duke here keeping you up all night is he?" Riley winked again, wriggling his eyebrows

I felt awkward and shuffled my feet, looking down.

"Get out of it Riley" Duke joked as his grip around me tightened

"Anyway pretty" Riley began with his gaze on mine "I was wondering if you could call in sick tomorrow? Jaymi and I are going to spend the day at the lake, we haven't spent much time together, and wondered if you wanted to come"

"She has to go to school" Duke cut in for me

"The lake?" I asked, ignoring Duke

"The one we went to before the war with Ryde and Dodge" He reminded me as he rocked on his toes

"Sure" I smiled "I love that place" It probably wasn't a good idea, but I wanted to spend time with them.

"Rosie, no" Duke cut in again looking down at me sternly

"Duke, yes" I mimicked "But you'll have to drop me off at work at four" I added towards Riley

Duke sighed while Riley walked back upstairs "It's a done deal Rosalie Jean" He called, satisfied

"You're falling behind Rosie, you aren't going to pass and graduate if you keep ditching" Duke started when Riley had disappeared

"I can deal with it"

"You keep telling me how much you're struggling, you keep reminding me how far behind you are" He continued, sounding like my father once again

"You also let me sleep in way past my alarm, causing me to be hours late to class" I fought back, leaning up on my toes, placing my lips firmly down on his.

It worked, he surrendered into kissing me back, pulling me closer to his ice cold skin.

When morning came, I wriggled around in bed, feeling Duke's cold body beside me when I stretched out my limbs. My eyes groggily flickered open. At first sight, I saw Duke asleep beside me. He looked so extremely peaceful, his features soft. Bravely, I lifted a hand to trace his jaw line.Within seconds, his mouth slowly turned into a smirk as my fingers slid across his face.

"Morning" I grumbled

"Morning" He replied, his voice thick

My fingers lingered on his face, stopping when his hand caught my wrist, slowly kissing the bandage still wrapped around my hand.

"Do your hands hurt?" He asked, his eyes open

"No" I liedThey did.

"That's good" He stretched as he pulled me closer towards him so that half my body was ontop of his

"What time are Riley and Jaymi leaving?" I leaned up on my elbows

"About two hours, it's only eight" He answered as he stroked my hair from my face

I sighed and lay my head back down on Duke's chest, his muscles rising and falling

"Rosie, I was wondering if I could ask you something" Duke started.My heart began to race in fear of what would come next. 'I think you should move out? You should be closer to home? Will you quit work for me? ' My assumptions were countless and varied.

"Sure" I tried to sound unbothered

"Would you like to come with me to Paris during your holidays?" He slowly questioned, my mouth gaping open, my eyes widening

I turned my body towards him and stared

"Paris?" I asked, dumbfounded

"Paris" He repeated with a nod

"For how long?" My mouth twisted into a wide smile

"About two weeks"

"Just us?" I asked, nervous

"You, me, Jaymi and Riley"

"Paris?" I repeated again, completely bewildered

"Yes Rosie, Paris" He laughed

"I would love to!" I took his face in between my hands, pressing down hard on his lips with my own. He gave a laugh, kissing me back with the same amount of force.

I'd never been out of the country and if I was to have ever travelled, Paris would have been the first place. I was excited beyond belief, I wanted to shout it from the rooftops, post it on every social media account that existed.

"When will we be leaving?" I asked, pulling back from his face

"Next Friday afternoon" He replied.

I stared at Duke, mesmerised. He was amazing, the most perfect part of my life and I couldn't wait to share my first holiday experience in the city of love with Duke.

"Are you coming with us to the lake today?" I enquires as I got out of bed, stretching my limbs

"No, I have some things to sort out with Darius and Donald" He answered as I felt his cold arms snake around my waist while I stretched my arms upwards

"Oh" I sighed, somewhat disappointed

"I will never get sick of this place" I mumbled as Jaymi, Riley and I stepped out of the car to face the beautiful lake.

"Me either" Jaymi agreed

"What are we going to do for the day? Fishing? Picnic? Checkers?" I mused

She tapped her nose "We will be fishing yes. But no picnic and checkers, sorry"

I shrugged "Oh well, at least I get one"

"Let Riley unpack the car, let's go" She linked her arm in mine, walking towards the dock

I inhaled deeply and took in the bitter salted scent that filed my nose. It was quiet and all that was heard were the few birds overhead chatting with each other.

Jaymi and I sat on the edge of the dock, our legs folded together while we heard and ignored Riley groaning and complaining from unpacking the car alone. Jaymi and I admired the view, looking out towards the calm light blue water, sparkling under the sun, glimmering the skies reflection.

"I've been meaning to ask you Rosie. Who is this Callum guy I'm hearing so much about?" Jaymi started, taking my attention fully

"What are you hearing about him exactly?" I asked, ignoring her question

She shrugged "Duke was talking about you hanging out with him a lot. Even asked Riley if he could keep an eye on the two of you when you would go out late with him"

"Wait, what?" I scoffed "Riley's been tailing us?" I asked, shocked at the news

"Just for the last couple of days" She shrugged casually "But you aren't supposed to know that, so don't say anything!" She pointed a finger at me.

I held my hands up "Okay" I lied. I was most certainly going to bring that little fact up with Duke later on.

"So, spill, who is he?" She asked playing with the wood planks beneath us

"He's just a friend that I work with" I put simply

"A friend?" She raised her eyebrows

"Yes Jaymi, a friend" I confirmed

She sighed and didn't ask any other questions about it, which I was grateful for.

"Duke seems to know something about him that I don't though. You wouldn't happen to know anything about that would you?" I asked, edging for truth.

She gave me a sideways glance "You got me" She gave in easily.

"Tell me what you know" I pushed, more of a demand

"Duke seems to think your friend Callum is an Angel"

I scoffed and tried to contain my laughter before turning serious again when Jaymi remained straight faced. "An angel?" I repeated

She nodded "Go on" I urged

"There are such things as Angels in this world, demons, Vampires, psychics, healers or cure's" She began "Angels are sent here to protect and save people, they stop people like us from taking people like you away from life"

"Are you serious?" I tilted my head

"I am. They are a huge threat when it comes to us" She started again "They are powerful and susceptible to all of our powers, just like you are. They are sent here by above to watch over someone who is deemed vulnerable or targeted. They swear to their superiors to protect their subject at any cost"

"And why does Duke think Callum is one of these Angels?"

"Duke knew his father. Callum's dad was apparently some high up Angel that attempted to intervene between he and Anna" She explained as she watched the lake ahead

"But, there's nothing he can physically do to seperate us, right?"

"They are very strong willed, they can manipulate people very easily. They are charming, polite and almost every Angel manages to entice their subject to safety. He will try everything within his power to turn you against us, against Duke"

"Well its not going to happen, if Callum is what Duke thinks he is"

"Just be careful" Jaymi warned before Riley came up behind us, juggling fishing rods and tackleboxes.

My brain had hit overdrive. There was always a chance that Callum wasn't an Angel. It seemed impossible, but it seems to make sense; he hated Duke from the moment he met him. He was charming and he was trying hard to seperate me from Duke. Maybe he knew, maybe he knew exactly who they were and what they were.

"Rosie!" Riley snapped as he wavered a fishing pole in my direction

"Sorry" I stumbled as I took the pole from him, weakly smiling while he raised his eyebrows at me.

"What are you thinking about?" Riley asked as he squeezed himself in between Jaymi and I

I shrugged "Stuff"

"Stuff like what?" Riley pushed again as he pulled the tackle box closer to his body

"Are there even any fish in this lake?" I asked, looking down at the water beneath the dock

"Of course there are" Riley sneered, handing me a small dead guppy fish as bait

I screwed my face up and took it as he showed me how to hook it into the fishing line.

Chapter Five

"The type of business that my parents do, it isn't really what you would call normal" He began

I didn't say anything, I just listened.

"Rosie, I don't want you to freak out or anything, but I want to tell you that, I know, I know what your boyfriend is" He said it slowly, confirming what I already somewhat knew.

I nodded, looking at my fidgeting hands in my lap "I sort of figured" I mumbled.

"You did?" He asked, surprised

"And I'm pretty sure I know what you are" I continued

"You do?" He spoke again

"An Angel?" I assumed, looking up at his unreadable expression

He was frozen, staring at me, and then he sighed, his expression dropping

"Who told you?" He asked, not looking at me

"A friend" I answered simply

"I'm that business opportunity aren't I? You're trying to take me away from them" I began, feeling angry at him

"Rosie, they are killers" He tried, staring at me

"You have no idea what you are talking about Callum" I started as I stood. He had no idea how much those 'killers' had helped me over the past year.

"Those 'killers' saved me. Numerous times. They have given me love, a family, friendship, everything I have never had before. Where were you when I was nearly killed? Where were you when my mother was killed? My father?" I continued

"I wasn't assigned to you back then, nor your parents, I didn't know about any of that" He defended as he stood up "None of it would have happened if you weren't staying with them. You should have left them, escaped with your life after the first incident" He continued

"You have no idea about my life, or anything to do with my life Callum. I have no one except them. They give me everything" I argued

"Like what? A fancy house? A handsome desirable Vampire boyfriend?"

"You know what? Forget it. I don't have to explain any of this to you" I attempted to storm off, but his strong grip grabbed the top of my arm, stopping me.

"I won't just forget it Rosie. I care about you"

I turned my head, but didn't look at him "You only care, because its a job for you. I'm just some exam that you need to pass" I spat

"That was before I got to know you, I care about you more than I should. You are an amazing woman and I hate to see you wasting your life away with those dead souls"

My blood boiled at his words. They weren't dead souls. Those dead souls made me feel more alive than what I actually was. I loved them.

"I'm in love with one of those dead souls thanks" I spat again

"Because you havn't known any other love Rosie" His voice was soft

I closed my eyes and sighed. I'd never thought about it like that. But I had had boyfriends before, and none of them ever compared to Duke. I was sure nothing would ever compare to him, I didn't want anyone else to compare to him.

"I love him Callum, and nothing you say or do is going to take me away from him, so if I was you, I would ask for a new project subject" I growled, keeping my voice low as I wriggled my arm from his grip.

"You aren't a project to me and you know it. I need to save you from this, not just for myself, but for you. You can have a normal life and be happy Rosie. Think about it. Does he struggle to keep himself in control when he kisses you, when he hugs you, when you bleed" I felt his hand reach out towards mine and take a hold of my bandages.

I kept my eyes and body faced away from him, ready to run.

"But he does control it, because he loves me back" I mumbled

"Do you want kids? A future? To become old and sit in a rocking chair, surrounded my small grandchildren and aging family? I can give that to you" He tried again, almost begging "He cannot"

"You aren't normal either Callum" I shot

"No, I'm not. But I have a heartbeat, warmth, blood, feelings, a future" He continued quickly

"That doesn't matter to me" I stumbled. Of course it mattered, but I couldn't let him know that.

"It does. I know it does" He caught me out

"I can't handle this right now" I stumbled storming out of the yard, back into the kitchen, through the restaurant, past Malory and straight to my car.

I felt my eyes sting, burning as I drove home. I cried because I thought my life had finally turned a page, turned civil, and then an Angel came barging in, asking for me to choose him over my Vampire boyfriend. I was confused and I didn't know how to deal with all this new information. I couldn't tell Duke what had happened, as far as he knew, I had no idea about Callum and what he was.

I tried to push the tears in my eyes back, ignoring everything that had just hapened, but it was difficult. Luckily, I had had an hour to contain myself, cry my eyes out before I got home to Duke. All I had ever wanted was a normal happy life, sure, Callum could give that to me, but my heart was with Duke.

By the time I made it down the street towards home, my eyes were dry and drained. I could hear my phone in my bag ringing, but refused to answer it in fear of it being Callum.

I pulled the car up out the front of the house and flipped down the mirror above my head. I looked over my appearance, pressing down on the redness of my eyes. I took a deep inhale and exhale before stepping out of the car, my mobile phone ringing again inside my bag. I headed towards the house where Duke swung the front door open, standing still in the doorway waiting for me.

"Afternoon gorgeous" He smiled a dazzling set of teeth when I reached him

"Morning" I joked, coming out shaky

"Are you okay?" He asked, his eyebrows slowly creasing as he stepped down towards me, tilting my head up for him to examine my face.

"Yeah, just had a rough day at work" I shrugged, brushing it off casually

"You've been crying" He noted as he looked at my swollen red eyes

"Yeah, Thursdays are busy, crowded, full of hormonal teenagers" I lied again, even though it was half true

He seemed to shutter at the thought, weakly smiling at me as he pulled me inside and into his arms.

I wrapped my arms around his torso and held on tight, fearing my eyes were going to let loose once again. I squeezed them shut and held on for dear life, guilt riddling into me for lying to him.

Chapter Six

Work was awkward, for the first time in a long time. I was suddenly grateful that there were so many customers around to keep me busy and out of Callums way. He knew I was avoiding him, and I was sure that at some point he'd stop me and demand to talk. I knew it was going to happen, but the longer I could put it off, the better. I wasn't sure how to process all of the information, it was drowning me. My head was pounding, my eye sockets sensitive to light, my vision occasionally blurred.

It was nearly midnight and I was looking forward to going home, crashing out beside Duke. Mentally, physically, I was exhausted, I needed the safety of slumber to heal me.

"Rosie, I'm not going to give up on you that easy" Callum spoke softly towards me, snapping me from my pained trance. I sighed behind the kitchen counter a few steps away from him.

I chose to ignore him, waiting for him to make the last order of the night.

He didn't say anything else, continuing to rush the meals that I was waiting on, probably eager to start interrogating me.

A few minutes later, he handed me the plates, making sure his fingers brushed against mine as he did so.

I rolled my eyes and moved towards my customers, handing them their meals with a wide grin before returning to where Callum stood.

"Whatever you want to say, say it now, and quick, I want to go home on time" I mumbled as I stacked the dishwasher

"This isn't a joke" He shot as he glared at me sideways

"Its beyond a joke" I scoffed as I looked at him, leaning my hip on the bench

He shook his head, frustrated.

I didn't say anything else, I just waited for him to continue, but surprisingly, he didn't say anything.

I thought I had won the battle, but I was wrong. With my bag on my shoulder, I made my way out towards home after lock up.

"See you Monday" I waved at Malory who aimed towards her ink blue Mazda

"See you Monday" She repeated

Unlocking my car door, pulling it open, Callum appeared behind me. I jumped and held my heart, startled

"Don't sneak up on me like that" I shot, dumping my bag into the passenger seat

"Hang out with me tomorrow" His tone changed

"Hang out with you? Why would I want do that?" I asked facing him

"Because I want to make things right. We don't have to talk about our situation, we can just hang out, watch a movie, have coffee, have dinner, like friends do" He trailed off slowly, casually

"Are you serious?" I scoffed, astounded

"I'm serious" He nodded

There had to be a hidden agenda.

"Look, I appreciate it, but I think I need a little more time to process all of this information" I waved a hand over his figure as I spoke

"Do you think it's perhaps because you're afraid that you'll realise the inevitable" He continued as I rubbed my forehead in frustration

"No Callum. I can't handle anymore drama, and you, you're drama" I said, pulling my car door wide open again, ready to get inside

"Just come out with me tomorrow" He tried again stepping closer towards me

I didn't want too, but I wondered how long he would try and how long I could fight him off for. We worked together, I saw him often, the longer I held off, the more awkward I would make it. "Fine" I finally gave in "But we aren't going to talk about you being what you are, we aren't going to talk about Duke and we aren't going to talk about my love life, understand?"

"Was that so hard?" He smiled smugly

"Yeah, it was" I muttered

"Despite this mess, we are still friends, you can't deny that in that sense things work well" Callum tilted his head sideways.

It was true, he was my friend, and despite all of this, I did want to stay friends with him. He was good company, safe company. He was charming and something about him made me feel somewhat normal.

The drive home was traffic free, quick. I was glad there had been no bickering and arguing. I was glad that Callum wasn't pushing the 'stay away from Duke' topic. There was doubt in my mind that he would continue trying, but there was no way I was going to give in.

When I got home, Duke was in his usual spot, leaning casually on the doorway when I got out of my car. Instinctively, I smiled at the sight of him. No matter how many times I saw the man, my heart still reacted the same as the day I had discovered my feelings for him. My attraction would never change for him, and that made me confident that I could conquer anything Callum threw my way.

"Hey" He greeted as I walked up to him, wrapping my arms around his neck, my lips on his a little too forceful that intended

His body stiffened for a moment. I had caught him off guard, but soon he joined with the same force that I was pressing against him. Duke was all I had at this moment in time. He was the only part of me that felt completely right. He was my rock, my diamond in the rough.

"Nice to see you too" He breathed when I pulled away

Chapter Seven

"How old are you, really?" I asked, walking through the dimly lit park with Callum

We'd watched a movie before heading to lunch, chowing down on Italian. We'd chatted for a good few hours about small things, but now I wanted to get serious. I wanted answers and serious ones about our serious issues, despite tell him that I hadn't wanted to discuss them.

We were strolling aimlessly in the park, side by side as I watched the landscape ahead of me.

"You really want to know?" Callum asked, raising his eyebrows after he smiled "I thought these conversational things were out of bounds?"

"I know I said that, but, there are things I need to know to better understand the situation I'm in, so yes I do really want to know" I answered, glancing at him sideways

"Okay then" He sighed "Ninety Three"

I stopped walking and stared at him, my mouth slightly hanging open

"But for earthly conditions, I'm twenty. The rest of my years were shaved off for the amount of people I have helped"

I quickly calculated it in my head, that would mean he'd either saved 73 people over his lifetime, or killed 73 Vampires.

"Wow" I nodded, narrowing my eyes in the distance, walking ahead again

"Its not that many if you knew of some of the ancient Angels that exist" He proudly informed, keeping his stride even with mine

"Well, I don't. I only know you"

"I can introduce you to some if you'd like, my parents would love to meet you too" He smiled, following my gaze up at the tree tops

"Maybe another time" I half joked, not wanting to meet them at all. I knew what meeting the parents would mean, or do. It would suck me in further to his world where trickery gave them the upper hand.

"I understand" He nodded, looking at me quickly again "So, is there anything else you'd like to know?"

I pondered for a moment before speaking "How many Vampires have you killed?" I asked, my face turning serious

His smile vanished and he sighed "You don't really want to know that"

I paused for a moment "Yeah, I do" I was nervous about it, but I needed to know who I was involving myself with.

"A lot"

"How many is a lot?" I asked, pushing for specifics

He sighed again and stopped walking, facing me. I stopped walking too, but didn't face him.

"I'm not sure exactly, over 30 maybe" He shrugged

I looked at the ground and shuffled my feet before turning to face him.

I couldn't help but scoff an unamused smile, shaking my head as Callum watched in confusion

"I shouldn't even be talking to you. My boyfriend and my friends are all Vampires, and you, you are a Vampire killer. It's just, so wrong" I half laughed, no humour whatsoever involved

Callum looked in between me and the ground, his hands shoved deep in his pants pockets. "Just so you know, aslong as your with him, I wouldn't hurt him" He spoke, watching me carefully

"And if I wasn't with him?"

"He's fair game" Was all he answered with.I knew in other words, he'd kill him.

"Why wouldn't you kill him when you have the chance, whenever I'm with him you could do it?" I asked, curiously

"Because it would hurt you if I hurt him" He answered, his eyes soft and gentle

I smiled and looked at the ground shuffling my feet awkwardly

"You know, I used to wish my life was normal. Sometimes I still do. I used to wish that I had a mother and a father that were lawyers or bus drivers, that they could ground me when I snuck out at night to go to a party with my friends. A brother or sister to keep me from breaking when the boys at school broke my heart. The normal boys that had normal lives, the ones that would take me out on dates, kiss me in the car, walk me to my door where my dad would yell at me for being out so late" I paused before continuing "But instead I have this mess of a life. One that I haven't chosen, one that I was born with which automatically makes me a target. I've nearly died at the hands of Vampires, on numerous occasions. I've fallen in love with one, I've become great friends with some. Now, I find out one my friends kills them, because he's a ninety three year old Angel" I admitted honestly as his eyes searched my face

"You can go back to all if you wanted" Callum began, never moving his eyes from my face "You can find an apartment to rent, go to school, hang out with your friends, date boys, save your money, go travelling, be a teenager. A normal teenager" He spoke, his voice soft and calm

I shook my head "Can I though? Knowing what's out there? Knowing that I will always be looking over my shoulder? Besides, I've gained a lot from what I have now too, could I throw all that away?" I mused walking towards a park bench, sitting down

"Its a difficult choice, and one that I can't make for you, but I want to help you decide, help you choose the right one. I don't want to see you get hurt Rose, I don't want Vampires to know who and what you are. I don't want to ever have to take action because you chose to become one of those beasts" He sat down closely next to me

"Take action?" I questioned, creasing my eyebrows

His expression was pained as he lifted his gaze to mine "If you become of them Rose, I'll have no choice but to treat you as I do them, as to what you are to us"

"Well, you don't have to worry about that. It'll never happen" I assured him, watching as he half smiled with relief

"At the end of the day, I just want you to be happy" He smiled, placing a hand on my knee "But for the right reasons, without doubt, without fear"

I felt a surge of current run up my leg from his touch, it quickly made me feel uneasy. Uneasy because it felt nice, comforting, safe.

"I appreciate it Callum" I smiled, keeping my eyes on his hand that remained on my leg

"Can I ask you something, personal?" Callum cut through the silence, his eyes avoiding mine

I nodded, watching him carefully

"Do you feel anything towards me? Apart from a friendship?" He dragged out the sentence slowly

My palms began to sweat, my ears ran hot. I did have feelings for him, but it was wrong. It was betrayal. I loved Duke, he was my boyfriend. I wanted to turn the question on him, but I already knew the answer. I was backed in a corner.

"I never thought it was possible to have feelings for two very different people" I moved my eyes down to his hand still lingering on me

The corner of his mouth lifted as he got the answer he was looking for. "I guess you get the normal teenage boy problems in the confusing sense you wanted it" He lighly joked squeezing my knee

I returned his smile and bravely looked back up at him. He was staring right back at me, and the sudden proximity of his face near mine made my heart jump. I should have moved away, but I didn't, I felt my skin crawl. His eyes were searching mine as if asking for permission, but I couldn't move, I couldn't breathe. I was closing in on giving intimacy to an Angel, while dating a Vampire. It felt wrong, confusing, yet something pushed me forward, edging me to do it.

Chapter Eight

The last week of school and work had went fast. I kept my head down, my night's strictly filled with homework. I didn't go out, I didn't work overtime, I did what I had to do to finish the work from school before leaving for my holiday. I was looking forward to the trip, but I wasn't looking forward to the reaction I was sure to get from Callum. I hadn't mentioned it to him yet, and I had demanded that Malory didn't say a word to him about it.

Friday went by in a blur. After school, Clora hugged me repetitively, demanding for me to call her everyday and take loads of pictures to show her when I returned. She was just excited as I was, and almost acted as if she was coming along too.

I hadn't stopped thinking about the trip all week, but my excitement faded as I drove to work. I had taken the afternoon off, but I wanted to tell Callum up front in person before I left tomorrow morning. I'd at least get a night of recovery from the fit he was sure to have.

Things between Callum and I had intensified, but not in a good way, the awkward way. Thankfully, he never pushed the kids that had occurred, and nor did I. I didn't hover, and I didn't stick around longer than what I needed too, I just did what I had too and moved on.

"Afternoon" Malory greeted as I walked into the warm establishment

"Afternoon" I replied, a smug excited smile playing on my lips.

"Excited I see" She commented as I slowly walked past her

I nodded and made my way to the back of the kitchen. I felt my palms sweat, my skin shiver. I could hear Callum's radio playing, but it fell on deaf ears, Callum wasn't there.I moved out the back door, walking towards the small dark yard. My heart dropped when I saw his back turned to me, his body perched on the wooden table in the centre of the yard.

Slowly I walked towards him, conscious of the crunch the leaves made beneath my feet. Callum spun around and I was surprised to see him holding between his fingers a cigarette. Throughout the time I had known him, not once had a seen him smoke.

I looked inbetween him and his hand as he noticed

"It helps with stress" He lightly laughed putting out the butt with the tables end, tossing it into the bushes.

"It creates stress, especially on your lungs" I shot back, half smiling as I moved towards him, sitting down on the table, my feet on the seat

He scoffed and stood in front of me, watching, waiting. I took that as my time to speak and bravely outed the words.

"I came by to let you know that I will be having 2 weeks off" I started, easing the topic up

"2 weeks?" He repeated watching me

"I'm going away, a little holiday" I answered casually, shrugging.

"Where too?" He edged, getting closer to the big argument

I looked at the ground and shoved my hands deeper into my jackets pockets

I sighed, "Paris"

"Paris?" He repeated, his voicing raising a little

"Paris" I confirmed looking up at him

"That's a bit more than a little holiday" He scoffed

"I guess it is" I smiled, suddenly feeling as though it wasn't going to be as bad as I had thought

"Are you going with them?" He continued on specifics

"Who else?" I replied, knowing he was going to become uncomfortable with the fact I was going with Duke and the others

"I should probably tell you its not a good idea and you shouldn't go, but you're just as stubborn as I am, and it really wouldn't do anything to change your mind" He started, taking a seat beside me on the table.

I smiled, knowing that no argument would erupt tonight

"But I'm going to warn you, Paris is a hot spot for rogue Vampires" He continued as I kept my eyes on my feet

"Rogue?" I asked.

"The vampires that don't care about the law, including their own laws. They take one whiff of you and they will know your something special, something, different"

"I've come across other Vampires before, and they had no idea I was different" I shrugged

"Have you?" He asked, not believing me

I thought about it for a moment. He was right, I hadn't met any Vampires that weren't aware of my condition.

"They'll know as soon as they smell me?" I asked, curious yet frightened

"If they get close enough, yes" He answered, causing me to cringe

"Well, they aren't going to get close enough, I'm going there for a holiday, to relax, sightsee, that's it" I defended

"Are you sure that's the only reason?" He asked, narrowing his gaze, his eyebrows raised

"What other reason would there be?"

He sighed and looked ahead into the distance "You should ask him, ask him what the real reason is"

"Tell me what you think the real reason is"

He shrugged "Ask him Rose"

I was about to beg again when Malory burst out from the back restaurant door "We have hungry customers Cal" She spoke, poking her head out at us.

"I'm on it" He nodded towards her. He hopped up from the table and began to walk back, turning his head towards me as he reached the door.

"Have a nice trip. Stay safe" He weakly smiled before leaving.

Chapter Nine

The plane ride had been as expected, incredible. The entire time, I sat in my chair, watching the clouds outside drift past, feeling the constant to reach out. For a few minutes, towns whisked past below, and then it became harder the see. Landscapes of mostly green and blue became the main focus, equally as beautiful, fields of natural life.

After hours of eagerly sitting forward, looking out of the window or chatting with Duke about our plans, I felt a wash of hype begin when the plane began to descend. My eyes were sore from the amount of times I had forgotten to blink, my back aching from the uncomfortable position I'd remained in. I was keen to exit into new adventure.

"Where are we landing?" I asked waiting for the roads and town to appear

"A small private landing strip just outside of town"

I turned my head back to the window and watched as the plane became lower and lower, eventually edging close to the visible tar landing. There was but one building on the area and another two small planes. I watched and felt my hand grip the seat as we fell, the tyres of the plane lightly brushing against the ground.

Soon, the plane came to a complete stop and I felt myself sigh. We had arrived. Here I was, in Paris. I smiled to myself as Duke got up "I'll meet you outside" He told me before walking back towards the pilots area again

"Lets go" Riley jumped as he pulled up from his seat, followed by Jaymi who linked her arm with mine, pulling me up from my seat to exit the plane. I felt my legs wobble and my vision blur, so I naturally took more of a hold on Jaymi. She had noticed my unsteady condition when I could hear her asking me what was wrong, the sound ringing. Immediately, I felt my body rely on jaymi a lot more than normal to remain upwards.

"Dizzy" I waved, barely audible, slurred. I tried to regain myself when we were greeted with outside cool air, sucking it in when my lungs breathing constricted.

"My luggage" I stumbled again, distracting myself from the tightening of my chest

"It'll be taken to where we are staying, don't worry about it" She gently smiled as she moved me forward

"What's wrong with her?" Riley quizzed, unsure

"She's dizzy because she's been sitting down for so long" Jaymi replied, calm and unbothered "She hasn't eaten properly either"

"Humans" Riley muttered as I rolled my eyes, noticing my breathing and vision slowly return

"You alright?" Jaymi asked, turning her attention back to me

"Where are we staying?" I asked, forcing my body to forget it's poorly state

"One of Darius' complexes" She answered

"Complex?" I asked, creasing my eyebrows as Duke reappeared from the plane

"Yeah, one of those cute little risers with vines and flowers hanging from the windowsills" She continued with description

Jaymi led me towards a waiting car where I hopped in beside her and Riley. I closed my eyes as I settled my head against the leather seat.

"Your excitment seems to have worn off" Riley snickered as he looked me up and down

"I don't feel very well all of a sudden" I mumbled. I felt my stomach twist, forming knots that would pull and push on my intestines. My head was aching and I felt the need to throw up the lonely water and crackers in my stomach.

I tilted my head to squint out the window, darkness shrouding over the horizon. It was nightfall and a small part of me sighed in relief. The night gave me an excuse to crash out for a few hours, or more, when we arrived at the complex.

We had drive for about twenty minutes, until the car slowed down and pulled into a narrow street. The road patterned with light orange bricks. The sides of the streets were lined with houses, tall and near glued to each other. They were all similar, almost the same design when we pulled into a small driveway. The driveway sat at the end of the street, beside the last house which sat next to a small flowing river. There was just enough light from the tall street lamps to see the water gliding beneath a bridge connected by a footpath. It was within walking distance and I knew that it would be somewhere I would spend some time standing on during my stay.It was simple, yet beautiful.

When we had stopped, I saw Duke exit the drivers seat, followed by Riley in the back, then Jaymi, I followed her, pulling myself out slowly and gently as my stomach screamed in protest.

I walked ahead, following Duke and Riley, Jaymi walking behind me, probably ready to catch me if I fell. I was disappointed in myself for being sick. I wanted to enjoy the arrival, not matter what time of day or night it was. I didn't want to sleep, I wanted to explore the city even in darkness. I wanted to go with Jaymi to the cafe she talked about, I wanted to stand on the bridge I had spotted on the way in, but instead I felt my insides exploding with pain, almost doubling me over. I gripped my hand on a twisting metal hand railing lined up the porch steps for support, worried I wouldn't make it inside.

"Are you okay?" Jaymi asked as she noticed. Riley's head turned around in front of me, looking at me, his face concerned. Duke had been too busy unlocking the door, flicking through keys to notice, twisting the correct key into the door.

I kept myself straight and casual as I passed Duke walking into the house. It smelt strongly of wood, almost like a pine forest or the cabin I had stayed in. Riley flicked a light on and I was brought face to face with the small home.

The living room was quaint, simple and cosy. The lounges were vanilla coloured, matching the carpet. No television was present, only a small coffee table in the middle of the room, along with a fireplace off to the side, just like the cabin. The sudden bright light made my head spin, that's when Duke came up beside me.

"Are you alright?" He asked as he lifted a finger, placing it under my chin, angling my face up towards his. His gaze darted over my features, stopping on my eyes as my stomach took another churn "You've lost colour" He commented

"Yeah, I just feel a little sick" I admitted, knowing there was no way or reason to lie to him

"Maybe you and Jaymi should start your adventures tomorrow, you should eat something then get a good nights sleep, it was a long flight and your body isn't used to it" He spoke, never moving his eyes from mine

"Okay" I gave in" Weakly smiling

He moved his hand from my face, taking a hold of my hand by my side. He led me up towards a narrow staircase, the top dark and eerie as we edged closer upward

"Does your head hurt?" Duke asked, his hand practically dragging me forward

"Yeah" I answered, the darkness soothing for my brain.

Once we reached the top of the stairs he led me through the darkness, continuing with only a few beams of light from outside giving me direction. I continued in tail, following into a room the furthest down the hall to my right. He pushed open the door and pulled me inside lightly shutting it behind us. From the window to the far right, I could see the front of the street. I looked down and could see the lights hovering below, lighting the road with a glow, the water from the river to the left glistening.

I turned around and could see that Duke had turned on a small lamp, igniting the room with a soft glow of light. He moved towards me and drew the red curtains closed.

Turning, I took in the room.There was a double bed in the middle, neatly made up, the covers and pillows a crimson satin. I glanced around the room and noticed a single framed picture hanging on the wall opposite the bed. The frame was red and inside the glass, it held a photograph of the Eiffel tower, it was lit up with lights like a Christmas tree.

"This is where you'll be sleeping" Duke spoke, breaking me from my trance

"It's nice" I commented, the sudden thought of what he'd said registering.

"You're staying in here with me too, right?" I asked

Chapter Ten

"Ready to go?" Jaymi asked as I finished up my meal of bacon and eggs, my second serving.

"Sure am" I sighed, glad my stomach had been kind, so far

"Have fun" Riley called from the living room, his fingers tapping vigorously while playing his PSP

"Be good" Duke smiled as he leaned against the kitchen counter top watching me intently

"Never" Jaymi joked, linking her arm in with mine, pulling me away towards the front door. I gave Duke one last smile and wink before loosing sight of him.

"I'm going to take you for a tour around the streets, then when lunch comes I'm taking you to that adorable little cafe I was telling you about" She instructed as we walked outside into the crisp cool air. People were scattered about, soaking in the weather. Various people paused to look at us, almost as if sniffing the tourists out, or it could have been because Jaymi was beside me, model gorgeous.

"I'm glad to see you're all better today Rosie" She commented looking me up and down

"Me too" I smiled, letting her pull me forcefully upwards towards the bridge I had seen last night.

"This is so surreal" I daydreamed, looking over the bridge as we stepped on top. It was curved stone, the edges on either side strong and safe despite the age. Small lamps were situated on each end of the wall, classic and formal. The water beneath glistened a light blue, reflecting off of the sunlight above in a mesmerising way.

"It is isn't it? That's why I like it so much. It's almost like living a dream" She agreed as we stepped off the bridge entering another street where more people sprawled out, staring as we passed. Jaymi didn't seem to notice it.

"So, I know this is going to sound personal, but I'm going to ask anyway. What did you do to piss Duke off so bad this morning?" Jaymi asked as we passed two young children playing with a skipping rope

"He was angry?" I asked, my eyebrows creasing as I absorbed in the passing scenery

"His eyes said it all when he came downstairs" She continued, making me feel uncomfortable. It hadn't been anger, it was lust.

"Oh, that" I shyly replied, feeling stupid, searching my brain for a lie that would work

"Were you talking about Callum again?" She asked, half sighing as she raised her eyebrows

I didn't say anything, remembering Callum back home who I had forgotten about since landing in Paris.

"Never mind. I can feel its none of my business" She smiled, relieving me of my aching brain "See there, that's where Duke's father proposed to his mother" She pointed as I followed her finger towards a small cafe.

Its windows were large and slightly pushed open, allowing insiders a view of the narrow leafy street outside. On one section of the window were the words 'toujours l'amour' painted in white, steadily written in beautiful calligraphic text. Inside I could see wooden tables, round with white table clothes on top. Customers were seated inside, some young couples and others older couples. It was a lovers paradise, no hooligans in sight to disrupt the peace.

"What does it mean?" I asked, stopping outside of the windows, looking at the flowing exaggerated letters

"It means 'always love'. The owners wanted it to be remembered as a place that would always give love, and in return, receive love. It's always worked, it's kind of perfect. If I were to ever meet the right man, I would want him to pop the question right there" She smiled, proud of her knowledge

"It does seem perfect for it" I pondered, looking at the cafe and its beautiful interior. Jaymi nodded before shaking her head, pulling herself from her trance. I giggled and followed her when she began pulling me further up the street.

"Can I ask you something Jaymi?" I began, narrowing my eyes

"You know you can" She smiled

"How come you don't have a husband or a boyfriend?"

She shrugged "Just havn't found the right one yet"

"You have had boyfriends before right?" I continued

"I have yes. But none of them were very family orientated, or trustworthy" Her face was somewhat tense, her jaw twitching

"I know how you feel" I snickered genuinly knowing how she felt

"You do?" She asked, raising her eyebrows at me

I nodded as we came up to another bridge. This one was wider and beneath it was a dock, a canoe lined along with a small group of tourists waiting to aboard.

"I'm hoping it's not as bad as what I have been through" She continued

"That depends" I smiledWe stopped at a small wooden bench against an orange brick wall, taking a seat together

"Should you explain first or should I?" She half laughed, probably feeling the tension I did

I shrugged "I will" I wanted to make the situation easy on her, gain her trust, so I took the jump.

"I've had a few boyfriends before, they were all jerks, I mean, I'm young and the chances of them actually working were hard against me anyways. But it is one in particular that remains with me. His name was Nick, he had made a bet with his friends to date me, he was popular, handsome" I began, keeping my eyes ahead "I was so excited when he asked me out, a day later he got his friends to dump me, telling me that I had earnt him twenty bucks" I scoffed

"Then there was another, Kyle, he was smart, he genuinely took an interest in me, until he met Clora. One day he'd caught up with her by her locker, he tried to kiss her and told her that he didn't want me anymore, that he wanted her. She told me the next day and thankfully, I hadn't blamed her" I shrugged

"Finally, theres my Science teacher" I sighed, saving the worst for last

Quickly, her eyebrows creased "You dated a teacher?"

"No, no I wouldn't call it that" I started "I've briefly mentioned it to Duke, but it was during an argument so I'm not too sure he took it in. Mr Wilde, he was always a touchy feely sort of teacher, he got too close with most his female students and back then I was oblivious. One afternoon he asked me to stay back to chat with him, I had no idea what would transpire. The first few times, he'd just make jokes, make me laugh, make me feel comfortable with him, then he tried to kiss me, I pushed him back so he yelled in my face. He told me that if I told anyone, they wouldn't believe me. So, I didn't. I thought it was over, until.." I trailed off, remembering the scene in my head, shuddering

Jaymi put a hand on my knee in reassurance so I smiled and continued "He locked the classroom door, I tried to fight him off, but he was too strong, he was kissing me, fondling me. It was only when the school bell rang that he stopped before it could get any worse" I admitted, pushing away emotions as I spoke. She looked half angry and half upset, unsure of how to react in front of me.

"I'm surprised Duke hadn't focused on something like that" She watched me "I mean, it's hard for me to resist racing back home, finding his home and snapping his neck" She half joked

"Whens the last time" She trailed off

"Just after I moved in with you guys"

She appeared angrier than before "You should have told us Rosie"

I shrugged "It doesn't matter. It's over now" I smiled forcefully "Anyway, now its your turn"

Jaymi hesitated before she relaxed back into the bench, she stared ahead when she began

"I've had two serious boyfriends during my lifetime. The first was Damon. He was wonderful, everything I had always dreamed of, until he decided that girls weren't really his thing" She laughed "I mean, I always knew he liked shopping with me, but, I just thought he had good taste" This made my mood lift, my smile unforced.

"That's pretty bad" I laughed as she did

"The other was a Vampire named Casper. I thought that we were going to last forever. We were engaged" She smiled, looking up at the sky "We were a few months off being wed. Until one afternoon while attending the ladies room at our wedding venue, I walked in on my future husband, drenched in the lipstick of my bridesmaid hanging off his neck" My eyes widened.

"That's horrible" I mumbled looking at her "I'm so sorry"

"I'm not. I'm just lucky it happened before the big day" She smiled "I'm long over him, but it's something that will never leave my memory. It makes trusting someone again very difficult" She laughed standing up, holding her hand out towards me.

Chapter Eleven

"How was your day?" Riley inquired when we entered the house. He remained sunken in on the couch playing his portable game.

"Better than yours obviously" I shot

Riley's eyes fluttered up from his game, glaring at me "I had a very productive day actually, I have beaten all levels except the last" He smiled, acting like a small child

I snickered"Where's Duke?"

Riley shrugged, returning to his violent beating on the games buttons"Can you keep a secret?" He asked, his eyes darting back to me.I threw my body down on the lounge beside his "Probably not" I smiled, tilting my head sideways to look at his paused game

"Duke thinks an Angel has been sent here by Callum to look out for you" He grinned, whispering "So he went to spy"

"Duke is paranoid" I groaned "Callum didn't even seem to care that I was coming here"

"I don't really care either way" Riley replied holding his hands up "But it wouldn't surprise me if there was someone watching you from his end"

"Why? Because of the Rogue's?" I blankly asked. Rileys gaze turned hard on mine

"Callum should really learn to keep his mouth shut" He grumbled shaking his head

"At least he's telling me the truth" I shot back

"What he's telling you, you don't need to know" He quickly responded

I scoffed "Like the real reason you all brought me here?" I tried, hoping he'd spill about it without me having to ask. I'd pretended as though I already knew.

"And what might that be Rosalie?" He asked, his full attention on me.

Damn.

"You tell me" I tried being as serious as I could, folding my arms across my chest.

He snickered and shook his head before returning his attention back to his game. I scoffed in reply and stormed off into the kitchen. Why wasn't anybody willing to give me answers? If there was a special reason that I had been brought here, why not tell me? Duke knew what had happened the last time he had lied to me, was he willing to risk it happening again?

I felt angry, taking my frustration out on slapping myself together a sandwich with whatever ingredients I could find. I leaned on the counter top and ate my snack, trying to calm myself down. When I would begin to relax, my thoughts fought back. I was sure that when Duke came home, he would make some lie up about where he had been and it would only tip my anger off more. If Duke did decide to lie, I was going to call him out on it. I didn't care how much trouble Riley got into for telling me where he had really been.

When I heard the front door lightly close shut, I knew this was the moment of truth. I had finished my sandwich and stood ready. I waited, listening to Duke and Riley lightly talking with one another. Unfortunately, I couldn't make out their words. Finally, his footsteps became audible and he appeared in the kitchen doorway.

"Afternoon" He smiled walking towards me.I folded my arms across my chest so he instantly knew where I stood"What's the matter?" He asked, his smile vanishing as he noticed my obvious look of disdain

"Where were you?" I asked, sounding like a suspicious housewife

"Taking care of some things" He replied moving closer to me. I chewed the inside of my cheek and narrowed my eyes at him

"What kind of things?" I pushed as he stood directly in front of me

"Does it matter?" He asked tilting his eyebrows at me

"Duke" I started, lightening my stern glare. If I wanted him to be honest with me, then I had to be honest with him, and now was a good time to start "I know"

He gave me an unsure look before I continued

"About Callum"

"What about him?" He was playing stupid, testing to see which secret I knew. I rolled my eyes and unfolded my arms "I know what he is, he told me all about it" I cleared up

"He did, did he?" He continued, playing a game I was unaware of

"I know he's an Angel" I continued, making things more clear for him

His face remained tightly held emotionless

"So, again, where were you?" I pushed, wanting to hear the truth from his own mouth

He sighed before giving in "Making sure you weren't being followed, as well as taking care of some things of my own business" He replied giving me half what I wanted to hear

"No one is following me" I defended

"I was only making sure Rosie, for my own reassurance" He replied, softening my anger. At least now he was being honest, that was what I had wanted.

"What else has Callum told you?" He asked, looking down at me, almost afraid of what I knew

I shrugged "He kills Vampires, Vampires like you for your involvement with people like me. He's assigned to me because being with you is eventually going to get me killed"

Duke rubbed his head "I was afraid that was what was happening" He mumbled

"What?" I asked, watching him.

Chapter Twelve

I woke up the next morning feeling refreshed and normal, well, somewhat normal. Last night had almost felt like a dream, something that only my mind could have conjured up during a long hard sleep.

When my eyes opened, Duke was gone, which was a surprise. It was odd for him to not be there. I dragged myself out of bed and studied my hair with my hands, it was tacky and oily at the roots, so I headed straight to the shower.

The shower was as equally as refreshing as my nights sleep. I leaned my arms on the wall of the shower while the warm water washed over my body. It felt beyond repairing and I was sure I had been there for over an hour. I ran over what had happened last night in my head, reliving the images before turning the water off and hopping out.

I wanted to find out what had happened, and something told me Duke knew.

I threw on a pair of skinny blue jeans and a grey Tshirt and then began downstairs. I could smell the bacon and eggs cooking instantly. When I reached the bottom, Riley was there, cooking as I heard Duke and an unknown man talking in the living room.

"Morning pretty, you've arisen just in time, breakfast is ready" He offered as I walked towards him

"Thanks" I weakly smiled, taking a seat along the bench as he dished me the food.

"Who's in there with Duke?" I asked as I chewed a piece of bacon

Riley shrugged "One of Duke and Darius' friends, he's an elder"

"An elder? Why is he here?" It had to of had something to do with what had happened last night.

"Because you my friend are amazing, but scary all at the same time" He overdramatised a shiver, leaning forward on the bench with his arms.

I stopped chewing and stared at him.

"Relax" He gestured waving a hand "You're extremely rare and extremely interesting"

"I think its weird, and it hurt" I replied

"Once you learn how to control it, it won't hurt as much, at the moment its kind of like an out of control remote control car, you just gotta learn how to use the controller" He explained

"So you know what happened to me? You know what I am?" I asked, narrowing my eyes at him

He shrugged "Once you're done here, you're wanted in there. They have the answers you seek" He smiled smugly

"Should I be worried?"

"Not at all, Aldo is a good guy, super smart, super kind, super old" He assured me with a wink "Old people know everything"

I rolled my eyes "Could I be anymore of a freak than I already am? I mean, maybe I should just end my life right here right now"

"I can help, push you off the bridge, it would be a pretty thrilling yet beautiful way to go, although, I'm sure Callum and his homies would stop me, they're sort of obsessed with you" He joked, easing my tension

I scoffed "What I do with my life is none of their business"

"Try telling them that" He snickered back standing upright.

I finished my meal and made my way cautiously towards the voices of Duke and Aldo. When I entered the room, the men stopped talking, both looking at me, standing.

"This must be our beautiful Rosalie" Aldo greeted, his voice gruff and aged. He was tall, but hunched. He had a small grey beard and moustache, the hair on his head thinning and white. His eyes were a caramel brown as he watched me carefully. Within seconds I had noticed. Aldo was human.

"You must be Aldo" I smiled as I held my hand out to the frail looking man. He took it with his skeleton like fingers gently squeezing before letting go.

I sat beside Duke opposite to Aldo as he sat in front of us.

"I hear you are quite the extraordinary young girl" Aldo started as he smiled

"If that's what you like to call it" I scoffed, unsure as I weakly smiled

His crazy eyebrows knotted together in the middle as he looked at me "Well, I suppose it is in order that I should tell you what you are" He started, clasping his frail pale fingers in front of himself. Duke was quiet beside me as I listened intently.

"I was once a vampire" My eyes widened slightly "I had lived that way for over two hundred years. It has been about eighty years ago now that I have been cured of my Vampirism" "Cured?" I asked, it sounded somewhat connected to what I was a Cure. Aldo nodded. "I had met a young girl, who like you, had a gift. She was exquisite and quickly became very well respected for her selflessness when it came to, our condition" He explained carefully "She was very well protected and had the respect of many, including that of Royalty. Her gift was seemingly the exact same as yours. The gift of the mind, where she too, was able to project her mind elsewhere while her body remained motionless"

"Where is she now?" I asked. Whatever fate this woman had endured, I was sure to endure too.

Aldo's eyes turned soft, and I knew right there and then she was long gone.

"There were a wide group of Rogue Vampires that weren't happy about her curing of others. The Rogue's thought that a Vampire wanting to become human was an opportunity for other pathways. They wished to turn vulnerable weak Vampires into soldiers. They saw what she was doing as a waste of a possible army of uprising" Aldo explained thoroughly

"They killed her?" I assumed

Aldo slowly nodded "It took them many years, and it was a bloody war to get to her, but they managed"

"Do they plan the same fate for me? Even though I'm not curing anyone? Do they even know that I exist?" As far as Dodge knew, I was dead, but he now appeared to be a minority. "Why haven't the Rogue Vampires killed Dodge? He plans on using my plan to turn others human.."

"It appears that Ryde had opened up to a few Rogue's about you before he was killed. And as for Dodge, they have been on the search for him over the last few years for his plans for you and your blood"

"Will they kill Dodge once they find him? That could be a good thing right?"

"They could, or they could convince him to join their ranks. Dodge wants power, becoming a part of the Rogue superiors would be all too tempting for him, he could be of great value for his knowledge to the Rogue's"

I leaned back shaking my head "I'm as good as dead"

"If they do start looking for you, I'll know about it. Duke has also informed me that you have case of Angel fever" Aldo continued "With the Vampires that you already know and the Angels you already know, this could turn out to be a good thing" He pointed out"If and when the Rogues decide to act, we'll have double the power, double the protection, double the chance of stopping them" Duke finally spoke up

"Do we realistically have a chance of beating this?"

Aldo and Duke nodded. I nodded slowly back.A war between good and bad in the Vampire world was erupting, and here I was right in the middle of it.It was then that I realised that for this to work, Duke and Callum needed to get on, they had to work together, for me.

"So, with this head thing that happens, does it just happen whenever it feels like it, or is there a way I can control it?" I asked, wanting as many answers as I could get

"You can control it of course. But there will be moments when your brain will want to take you somewhere you're unaware of because it wishes for you to see something you need to see. If there is somewhere you wish to be without being noticed, all you have to do is concentrate, breathe, and it should come naturally"

"Is it supposed to hurt so bad?" I asked, remembering the amount of pain that had surged through my brain

"The pain will stop when you learn how to control it. Its just a matter of concentration, the more you do it, the more experienced you will become at it" Aldo spoke, his moustache dancing

"I don't know if it's a good or bad thing that I can listen in on conversations that are probably being kept from me for a reason"

Aldo smiled almost "Yes, I suppose you are right. But with a clever mind, it can be cleverly used" He continued exactly like the old wise man I had expected.

Unfortunately, my power wasn't something I could physically use, not to fight, not to defend. It would need to be used more strategically, more planned and thought out. I was more a mental weapon than anything else. I was an old, outdated model of Seth.

It was easy to send that Duke didn't like the thought of me being able to intrude on places he didn't know about it. He was trying to protect me from Vampires and the deep dark secrets within, but now, I could know them all with the squeeze of my mind.

Chapter Thirteen

I'd taken many pictures during my day out with Duke, and I couldn't wait to upload them once I'd found and charged my laptop. I couldn't wait to show Clora, brag about all the beautiful things I'd seen.

Duke had taken me to original buildings, guiding me and informing me of each historical beauty's past and present.It soon became clear that he was leaving the Eiffel tower until last. I'd taken pictures of the rivers, lakes, buildings, the romance of the locals, even the small flowers hanging from vines off of buildings. I found even the most subtle of beauty, capturing it for my memories with pride. I'd even snapped a few secret shots of the cute boys that roamed around for Clora of course.

Altogether, I'd had a great day.Thankfully, there was no more talk of Callum, Angels and the future dangers that threatened my life. We talked about the weather, the City, home, Riley, Jaymi, Clora, other places we wished to travel together.Our next destination was Ireland and I clung to the hope of the idea.

We dawdled back home when the sun began to set. When we reached home, the only light came from the lamp posts that stood tall and dim at the sides of the streets.Duke and I walked hand in hand, quiet as only few people drifted outside. There were many lovers out at this time of night, lips interlocked as they stood against the bridges and houses. It made me smile, but I couldn't help but feel disappointed. I wished that Duke and I could have lost ourselves like those couples did. It wouldn't ever be that easy.

Once we were inside, Jaymi and Riley could be heard laughing together in the kitchen. I took the camera off of my neck and let go of Duke's hand, placing the camera down on the coffee table.Duke walked ahead towards the laughter with me soon following. As duke entered, I noticed the laughing fade down, interrupted by Duke.

The minute I entered the kitchen, I became suspicious. There was Riley and Jaymi, standing awkwardly beside each other, their hands behind their backs as they subtly licked their lips. I knew then and there that they had been feeding on blood. As soon as I realised it, I turned back around and left the room, my stomach churning.

"Ew" I mumbled as I headed upstairs towards my room. Despite knowing they needed blood to survive, it never ceased on grossing me out. Every time I thought about Duke drinking another human's blood, I felt a snippet of jealousy, uneasiness and wide repulsion.

I flicked on the room lamp, illuminating the small space in a dull yellow glow. I sat on the bed and pulled my shoes off, tossing them across the room as they landed with a light thud. I sighed and pulled the hair band out of my long ponytail, letting the strands fall loose around my shoulders and back. I placed the hair band around my wrist, lying down on my bed, sprawling out.

I closed my eyes and thought about testing my power using intense concentration. I wanted to hear the scolding duke would most likely be doing downstairs, but I decided that now wouldn't be the time, nor the reason to channel my ability. Minutes later, Duke had come into the room as the door creaked open and shut again. I kept my eyes closed and lay still, curious as to what Duke was going to do if I didn't react. I heard him sigh, trying to make his presence known. I didn't move, the corners of my lips turning up, waiting for him to react.

"Did you yell at them real good?" I asked

I heard Duke lightly snicker "I did"

"They do need to eat, I can't let myself stop them" I shrugged, peeling one eye open to look up at the tall proud man. He was standing right next the the bed, his arms shoved in his pants pockets as he looked down at me. I couldn't help but smile uncontrollably at the sight of him. He truly was the most perfect being I had ever seen even when it was almost dark.

"Are you going to move over?" He asked

"What do I get out of it?" I asked, raising my eyebrows as I shut my open eye again

I heard him sigh. I had expected a smart remark back, but instead, I felt the weight of him on the bed beside while I remained taking on the shape of a starfish.

I kept my eyes closed, shivering at the idea of what he was going to do next. I waited, and a few seconds later, I felt his fingertips trail up the skin of my arm. Goosebumps rose under his touch, my lips twitching upwards into a smirk. Strongly, I refused to open my eyes.

Without a bigger reaction, he continued to trail his fingers up my arm, reaching my shoulder, then my neck. He slowly slipped his hand underneath the back of my neck, his coldness rushing through my skin. I didn't move, but it was becoming extremely difficult. I then began to feel Duke's breath on my face, slowly it became more forceful, closer. I knew what was coming, and soon, his lips were lightly on mine in a matter of seconds. He was slow, calm, ever so gently brushing his lips on mine. I found myself falling for his spell. Every time I pushed for more, he pulled back, lightly laughing as he teased me. Eventually, I needed to open my eyes, look at him and see his expression for myself. It was still daring, seductive, his eyes remaining a light gold. My eyebrows creased slightly, surprised he remained in control of his temptations.

"Working?" He asked, leaning over me with his body careful not to place any pressure on me.

"A little" I smiled, biting my bottom lip

"At least I'm getting somewhere" He smirked with a shrug, proud of himself

"Tease" I mumbled gripping the neck of his shirt, bringing his face close to mine, crushing my lips to his. He smiled against me and I melted beneath his lips. We were testing each other, and I knew that eventually he'd pull away. His eyes were slowly getting darker and it was just a matter of time before the moment would be torn from us. With limited time remaining, I bravely pulled on his shirt, harder this time. I did what my body wanted, kissing him, not letting up when my breathing hitched. My breathing stopped when I felt Duke's body fall lightly on mine. I could sense that his control was slipping. I felt his chest on mine and smiled, roughly biting down on his bottom lip. And that was it. Instantly, he pulled his face away, his hand touching where I had nibbled. He looked at me, surprised at my bold move. I smiled proudly, enjoying the rare expression on his dumbfounded face.

"What? Its okay for you to bite people, but it's not okay for me to do it back?" I teased, realising what I had said had been grotesque.

I took his spare hand and dragged it up to my chest, placing it gently down where my heart was beating erratically. He watched and listened, and as soon as his hand felt my pulse his eyes turned charcoal. He could feel the blood flowing with each pulse of my heart beat, tempting him in more ways than one.

"I can feel your every flow of blood" He mumbled, watching me with his dark eyes

"What does it make you want to do?" I asked, half fearing the truth

He swallowed hard, his adams apple bobbing up and down before he ran his eyes over my neck. Thats when I knew that it made him want my blood, not my intimacy. Unarguably, my next move had been beyond irresponsible. I was risking my own life, for a game that I was taking too far forward.

I stretched my neck out wide, keeping my eyes on his as they trained on my neck. His eyes darted back to my face as it tilted upwards, testing his control at a dangerous level.

"What are you doing?" He mumbled, his voice low and struggling

"I trust you" I whispered back as his jaw tensed

"You shouldn't" He replied, dropping his face to my neck. I squeezed my eyes shut, waiting for the surge of pain when his teeth pierced my skin. I waited for the retract of fangs but it didn't come. Instead I felt his lips brush against my skin, pressing down as he kissed me. Relief washed over me and I smiled. He was in control.

My hands found the back of his head, I took fistfulls of his hair in between my fingers and pulled him closer. He trailed his lips up my neck until he reached my ear and then he stopped.

"You have no idea how tempting you are Rosalie, and I'm not talking about your blood" He smiled, his whisper brushing against my ear, making me shiver with delight

I woke up curled against Duke, his body cold and warm at the same time. I nestled my face closer to his chest, his arms wrapped around my body. He was asleep, I could hear him lightly snoring when my eyes flickered open. There was light gentle sunlight splaying into the small room, relfecting off the white walls.

I felt my nose begin to itch and burn, I was going to sneeze. I screwed my face up in an attempt to calm it, but it only made it worse. Unable to stop it, a loud burst of air flew out of my nose and mouth, waking Duke up instantly. He looked down at me, bewildered and drowsy.

"Sorry" I apologized as I sniffled, pulling away so I could see Dukes full features. Although he was still half asleep, he was smiling. I shook my head and sat up, rubbing my eyes free from sleep. Duke groaned and rolled over. I imagined him to be one of those men that dreaded leaving bed in the morning when he had once been human. He was the one you'd be throwing pillows at, yelling at to wake up at midday while the day wasted away.

I began to shuffle through my suitcase of clothes, pulling out a clean set. I made my way to the shower, smiling as I looked back at Duke who remained twisted in the sheets of satin.

After my warm shower, I headed back into the room. Of course, Duke was gone. I wasn't sure what was on the agenda for today, but I was curious, excited. I wondered if Duke was going to be taking me out again, or maybe it would be Riley or Jaymi. Either way, I was sure that today was going to be just as fun as the last.

I headed downstairs after throwing my hair up into a messy neat bun. Downstairs, Duke and Riley's voices could be heard from the living room. They were low, serious and I rolled my eyes. They were probably talking about my welfare and how much they hated Callum and Andrè.

I walked straight into the kitchen and opened the cupboard door to pull out a museli bar. I continued towards the living room, the voices becoming quieter, eventually stopping once I reached the archway entry

"You could at least say it to my face" I joked, taking a bite from my muesli as the boys both looked at me. Dukes face was serious, whereas Riley was happy, smiling at me.

"Bitching behind your back is way more fun" Riley stood up as he walked towards me

"I'm sure" I mumbled through chewing thick oats. Riley pinched my cheek as he walked past, causing me to swipe at his hand with my arms.

Chapter Fourteen

I realised I had been gone well over an hour by the time I got back home. I automatically knew that I was in for trouble when I met Duke inside of the house. His arms were across his chest, his face stern as he prepared himself for an argument.

Little did he know, I knew his secret. I knew why he'd brought me here, and it definitely wasn't because he wanted to take me on a nice vacation.

"Where have you been?" He asked, sounding like my father once again. I was getting pretty sick of him acting this way. I understood the protective boyfriend part, but this didn't feel like that. It felt like that moment when you had your first kiss and there stood your father waiting to tell you that the boy wasn't good enough for his princess. That, was what it was like.

"I could ask you the same thing" I shot back standing against the back of the door casually. I wasn't sure where I had pulled the smart remark from, but I was pissed. A large part of me, was sick of the secrets, lies. I was an independent woman, and I had every right to leave the house when I wanted, along with speaking to whoever I wanted.

"Don't be smart Rosie. You can't just go roaming whenever you feel like it" He replied, angrily

"Actually I can. I'm a big girl, I can look after myself. Beside, it's daylight, and I stayed within crowds, not in the forest with a sign above my head stating 'fresh meat'" I argued back, letting my inner demons out

"What has gotten into you Rosie? You know there are dangers around, you know just how easily you could be hurt. I understand that you think your invincible, but you aren't"

"You're not afraid of the Rogues Duke, admit it, you're only afraid of Andrè, and the Angels, so cut the danger charade" I shot back, interupting him

He gave me a sideways look, a look that said he knew I had been up to something he wouldn't agree with "Andrè?" He repeated, the anger in his eyes shining through

"Yeah, Andrè. That Angel you nearly killed, the Angel that happens to be honest. We had a nice chat today, me and him. Care to fess up before you spit out any more lies?" I edged, folding my arms across my chest as I leaned off of the back of the door

He unfolded his arms, and placed his hands on his hips, sighing furiously, attempting to keep his anger in check. He was having difficulties, I could see it.

"You shouldn't be fratanizing with the enemy Rosie" He spoke, his voice somewhat hushed as he controlled his emotions

"He's your enemy Duke! Not mine!" I yelled back, feeling the frustration boil in my blood "They are only looking out for me, and whatever beef you have with each other has nothing to do with me! Keep me out of it!" I let it all loose as he watched me, his eyes near black

He sighed, attempting to understand the truth in my words, mulling it over in his head

"Okay. Fine" He mumbled in between his teeth

"And the truth? Are you going to tell me upright or do I just have to take Andrè's word for it?" I asked, edging closer to the hidden agenda

"What truth?" He asked, obviously playing stupid to begin with

I rolled my eyes "Why did you really bring me here Duke?" I asked, my voice returning to the little teenage girl, afraid her boyfriend had betrayed her

He sighed again, and this confirmed his defeat

"Whatever he said, I'm sure its been twisted" He half whispered, his eyes returning to a soft honey glow

"Did you really bring me here because there was an Angel meeting, and you were afraid they'd take action?" I dangled the question in front of his face like a carrot in front of a horse

His eyes moved from mine, and seemed to falter. He had been caught out. And then it hit me, it was true, all of it.

I chewed the inside of my lip, refusing to let the tears spill in front of him. He didn't deserve to see me cry. He didn't deserve to see how much he'd hurt me.

"I thought we were over this lying business Duke" I whispered, my voice betraying me as it broke

He took a step towards me, lifting his hand to touch my face, but I yanked away, taking a step back as my body fell against the door again

"I'm sorry Rosie. But it wasn't the only reason I did want to show you Paris, I did want you and I to have a good time. I wanted you to be happy, and to have a good holiday, you've been so stressed lately, and I know I haven't been around as much as I should have. I wanted to make it up to you" He started to grovel

"You still lied" I managed out, watching him

"I know. I should have told you and I'm sorry, but I knew it would upset you, and you would say no to coming here solely for that reason alone. If you knew there was a meeting, you would think that was the one and only reason I was inviting you here, and it wasn't, it isn't" He continued, as one stray tear fell from the corner of my eye

"I'm sick of all the hate, the anger, the fighting, secrets, lies, its never ending Duke" I trailed off, wiping away a few more tears that forced their way out

"I know. I'm sick of it too, but sometimes, its what we have to do. Sometimes, its to protect the people we love, no matter how much it hurts" Duke continued as he kept his hands by his side, his voice even

I could just imagine how much he wanted to reach out to me, I could just imagine the pain he was feeling after I had found out that he'd once again lied to me. But I needed space, space to think.

"I need some space" I mumbled as I looked at the floor, not trusting myself to look into his eyes just yet

"I understand" He whispered back

I sniffled my running nose and walked past him, grabbing a few tissues from the kitchen before trailing upstairs to my bedroom.

Huddled into my sheets and blanket, I silently cried myself into a wet puddle on my pillow. I loved Duke, there was no doubt about it, but sometimes, I wished he was just as fragile and as human as I was. That way, things wouldn't have to be so dangerous, so hectic, so chaotic and dramatized. I wished it was me and him, in a small country village, where we lived in a humble little cottage surrounded by roses and colourful flowers.

With wishful thoughts in mind, I drifted off to sleep, the warmth of the sun outside coating me in security.

When I woke, I hoped it had all been a horrible dream. I hoped that I had awoken as someone else with a happy ending in sight for life. But I couldn't. I was going to have to deal with this for the rest of my life if Duke was who I really wanted to be with. How was I to manage at times like these?

I was sticky with salty tears that had wept out in my sleep. I wondered if the thoughts that rambled on in my head were ever to stop.

Slowly, when I calmed down, I realised it was dark.

I had slept for hours, which meant that I probably wouldn't be able to sleep tonight, and would have to deal with the awkwardness that would surely fill the house. I wished I was Jaymi. She seemed to have it so perfect. A small part of me wished that I was immortal as she was, that way, I would be stronger, I would be able to stand up for myself and not be worried about.

I quickly blocked my dangerous thoughts and sat up, looking around the darkness of the room. My legs were warm and tangled in with the satin blankets.

I ran my fingers through my messy hair, regretting it as knots pulled. It was then that an idea ran through my mind and I decided to act upon it. I closed my eyes and crossed my legs. I focused one thought in at a time and allowed my mind to relax, but wander. I concentrated hard, forcing myself to focus all of my attention into the living room downstairs. Slowly and surprisingly, I felt the soul of my body lift, drifting effortlessly into the living room. It was there where Duke and Jaymi were sitting.

I knew then and there, that my ability had worked successfully for the first time without pain being inflicted. I could hear and see what Duke and Jaymi were talking about without my body physically actually being there.

I watched intently and waited. Duke was slouched over, his head in his hands as he leaned his elbows on his knees.

Jaymi was watching him, her eyes concerned.

"Just give her some time" Jaymi reassured him

"I should have told her, it was wrong, I keep pushing it, I keep pushing the boundaries" Duke spoke, not moving from his position

"She loves you, she's angry, understandably, but she won't just up and leave" Jaymi continued as she lifted a hand to rest it on his back

"She doesn't deserve this, she doesn't deserve to be lied to, she doesn't deserve me as this beast" He mumbled as I leaned my face in, listening intently

"Let's not be dramatic Duke, I just think that from now on, you need to be honest with her, she's smart, and in the end she finds out the truth on her own. I know that sometimes lies are put in place to protect her, but we're going to find it harder to protect her if she decides to leave this life behind because of our dishonesty" Jaymi explained easily. She knew exactly what to say, she knew what my thought process would be like.

Jaymi knew me well, and I was glad she was there to give Duke advice. She was leading him in the right direction.

Duke didn't say anything, he just lifted his head. It was as his face came to view that I stumbled backwards, almost hitting the coffee table. In the corner of his eye fell a small amount of blood. What was wrong with him? I panicked and debated whether or not to return to reality.

Jaymi half smiled and touched the blood with her fingertip, wiping it away.

"I haven't seen you cry in awhile, and that's how I know she deserves you, because you care about her more than you have for anyone else" Jaymi smiled as she wiped the tiny drop of blood on her jeans

"I don't know how this works, I've never been at fault for a relationship falter. Do I wait until she's ready to talk, how do I smooth it over before it gets worse?" Duke mused as he leaned back wiping away whatever blood remained in the corner of his eye.

He was crying. Vampires cried blood. I already knew that for Vampires to show such emotion was difficult. Crying wasn't something they did, it was a rarity in their form. He really did love me that much, and it softened me to know.

"The next move is up to you. Just be sure you've given her enough space. Then it's all about being honest, tell her how you really feel, no more bullshit" Jaymi swore, shocking me. I hadn't heard her swear before, and it was strange coming from such a petite looking face.

Duke nodded before standing up and sighing.

Jaymi smiled as she leaned back on the couch, proud of her advice.I too was proud of her advice. This was why I loved her so much.

Realising where Duke was headed, I quickly concentrated on exiting my eavesdropping. Seconds later, the air dissolved and like smoke clearing under cold air, I was back in my room, sitting upright as my eyes widened open.

I pushed all emotion quickly from my expression, laying back down, facing the window that glistened with the moon's half wicked smile.

Not a second later, I heard the door creak open before shutting again. I scrambled my brain for a ready response when he would apologise, trying to make amends. I needed to be careful not to reveal my spying. I didn't want to forgive as easily as I knew I really wanted to. I needed to ensure he wouldn't ever betray me again.

I listened as he walked towards me, I felt the weight of his body on the space beside me. He just sat there, watching me as I dug my face into the drenched pillow.

"Rosie" He whispered, testing to see if I was awake or not. I decided to play it honest, just like what I wanted from him. It needed to work both ways

"Duke" I formally greeted, fighting back a smirk. No, I screamed at myself, I needed to be serious. This was serious.

"How did you sleep?" He asked gently

I shrugged

"I could send Jaymi up if you'd like someone to talk to" He continued, playing it cool

I knew how bad he wanted things to be forgiven and forgotten, I knew the desperation in his voice when I heard it. He couldn't hide it, no matter what he did.

"No. Its fine" I grumbled, lifting my face so I could look out the window as well as watch his face through peripheral vision

He was watching me, his hands kept inside his pants pockets, probably to refrain himself from touching me

"Is there anything I can get you?" He asked, his voice delicate

I turned my body around slowly and looked up at his face. It was still tinged with sorrow and regret. I couldn't be angry at him, not anymore, it was impossible.

I shook my head as he looked down at me, his eyes searching over my face

I sat up, dragging my sleepy limbs up with me. I sat with my legs crossed, bringing our faces close together again

"Promise me you won't ever lie to me again Duke" I whispered keeping my eyes on his golden orbs

"I promise you" He quickly agreed, taking his hands free from his pockets, obviously loosing the inner battle with himself

"Promise me you will stop acting like my father, and let me make some choices for myself" I continued

"I promise" He repeated again, watching me with the same intensity

"And last of all, promise me that you'll believe me when I say, I love you, and that will never change" I emphasized the never part, just to get it through to him.

Chapter Fifteen

It was about five in the morning when my phone began ringing. I was curled up on Duke's arms, playing with his hand in front of me, examining just how different we were in the most simplest of ways. His fingers were long, porcelain white, double my hand size. Mine were almost child like, petite, coloured lightly tan brown and visible veins blue and purple.

I sat up, pressing green on my phone and pressing it to my ear

"Callum?" I answered urgently

"Rosie? Hey! What's up?" He asked, excited

"We need to talk, it's urgent"

"Oh, kay" He slowly spoke, scared almost

"First off, you should have told me you were going to send someone to spy on me" I began full speed ahead "Second, you should have told me you were having a huge ass meeting, and third, you should have told me what they had decided. I want something done about it, you aren't going to take away the only family I have left, not without loosing me in the process" I demanded, sounding as forcefull as I could

He was quiet for a second, adjusting to the information before speaking

"Look, Rosie, I'm sorry about all that, I really am, I tried to talk them out of it, but it was no use, they see it as a huge opportunity" He started

"Callum, I'm telling you right now, if you don't do something" I racked my brain, watching Duke as he intently watched me listening to our conversation with his hawk like ears "I'm not coming back, at all" I threatened, making it up on the spot as Duke stared at me in surprise

"What are you talking about Rosie?" Callum spoke, angry

"I'm not going to let you take them away from me, I don't care who I have to hurt and who I have to leave behind. I will fight against you if I have too, so make the choice Callum" I spat, letting my wild side take over before I pressed the red button, hanging up on him.

Duke stared at me as I placed the phone down on the bed, lightly shaking at what I had just done. I'd just threatened my best friend, my Angel best friend for my Vampire boyfriend.

"That was intense" Duke smirked "Are you sure what you're doing is the right thing? I mean, I will understand if you want to sit on the fence here" Duke continued, fixing his sensible statement up

"I'm sure" I nodded

As I thought about it, my phone vibrated lighting up with a new message. I picked it up and read over the words, it was from Callum.

'Don't do anything stupid. I'll try talk to them. You have family here too Rosie, don't forget that'

I ignored it, and threw it aside beside the lamp

"What did he say?" Duke asked as I sighed, lying back down, staring at the ceiling

"He's going to talk to them" I mumbled, closing my eyes

"I can take care of myself Rosie, honestly, you don't have to do this" He assured me, his finger trailing lightly along my jaw line

"I know, but I need to" I whispered.

Surprisingly, while my adrenaline pumped, I had somehow managed to fall back to sleep. I wasn't sure if it were Duke's fingers, lulling me into comfort, tracing along my skin, or my mere mental exhaustion.

When I next woke, it was nine in the morning and Duke remained beside me, watching me.I smiled through fluttering eyes, and spent the next fifteen minutes embraced within him before finally, slowly, getting up.

I showered, taking extra time on my fuzzy hair and fury teeth before emerging downstairs.

Today, I had promised myself that I was going to have a good day. I was going to ignore the war that was brewing between the Angels and Vampires and just enjoy Paris like Duke had originally wanted me too.

He had agreed for Riley and Jaymi to take me to lunch at Toujours l'amour.

I'd grown to love the cafe and was determined to see at least one couple become engaged before I was to leave.

As we walked, I was aware that most of the people that passed us, practically stopped to stare. After all, there were three unbelievably gorgeous Vampires by my side, one of which held tightly onto my hand. I felt proud, proud that I was part of their group. It was like being in high school, holding the heart throb football players hand as you walked alongside your gorgeous loyal cheerleader friends. Naturally, I held my head up high as we entered the cafe.

We took a table towards the back of the restaurant, Jaymi and Riley sitting opposite me with Duke beside me as a familiar waiter approached us, notepad in hand as he stopped at the table, looking us over.

"What can I get you all this afternoon?" He asked, his accent thick like it had been when he had served Jaymi and I.

Once we had all ordered, we sat patiently and relaxed into conversation.

"So, I think its the right time to tell you both something" Riley started as he clasped his hands in front of himself

I chewed the inside of my cheek, knowing exactly what he was going to say. So did Duke, who refrained a smile.

"We know" I burst open, smiling, saving him from embarrassing himself

"You know?" Riley asked as Jaymi looked in between us both

"We know" I signalled between Duke and I "I happened to see you both making out, and Duke isn't as stupid as he looks" I teased nudging him in the side with my elbow as he smiled crookedly

"Oh" Jaymi replied for Riley as they looked down, embarrassed. If they had pumping blood, I was sure their cheeks would have been tomato red within seconds.

"I'm happy for you both" I smiled, easing up the tension

Riley and Jaymi both smiled and placed their hands together on the table. I leaned back in my chair, letting my hand fall on Dukes thigh.

It wasn't until I felt Duke flinch beneath my fingers that I realised the innocent gesture.

It was a simple intimate movement, but it wasn't appropriate when Duke had almost impossible self control. I quickly moved my hand and returned it to my lap before Jaymi or Riley could notice.

Duke's mouth slowly turned upwards in one corner as he looked away

I had to contain my own smile, just as the waiter returned with our plates of meals

I had ordered what I had last time, as had Jaymi. Duke and Riley both ordered hearty meals full of meat and pastry.

"I love this place" I spoke through chewing

"I do too" Jaymi agreed as we looked around "Maybe one day we can all get engaged here" Jaymi smiled while she day dreamed

Riley seemed to smile as he dug into his meal, I had also noticed him not so subtly give Duke a quick glance

I suddenly hoped that I would witness Riley propose to Jaymi. Despite the small timeframe that they had begun dating, I secretly wished for it.

"What do you think we should do after this?" I asked as I ate

"Whatever you want" Duke replied

"I want to go to the markets, I heard they were selling paintings this week" Riley spoke up, putting down his fork and knife when he'd finished up his entire meal before anyone else

"They looked pretty crap to me" I replied, remembering the paintings they were selling "We should go to the museum instead, there is some really lovely paintings there" I continued, remembering what Jaymi had shown me

"Sounds like a good idea to me" Jaymi agreed, taking my side. We all seemed to look at Duke, waiting for his opinion and final vote.

"I'm not getting involved" He smiled, holding his hands up in early surrender

"Oh, c'mon just agree to come to the museum with us" Jaymi groaned "You can't go against your own girlfriend, can you?" Jaymi cheekily taunted, raising her eyebrows.

"Hey, that's cheating" Riley objected

I refrained a giggle as Duke did, shaking his head

"Sorry Riles. She's right" He smirked, draping an arm over my shoulder. Jaymi and I smiled in success, winning our battle.

Riley rolled his eyes before shooting Duke a death glare "Traitor" He mumbled as we got up to leave, tipping the waiter for our food.

We strolled towards the gallery, watching the passing locals, admiring the lakes that flowed beneath the bridges we walked over.

I was hand in hand with Duke, Riley and Jaymi hand in hand in front of us. I couldn't help but smile at them. They were adorable together and I loved seeing them so happy with each other.It was what they both needed. Love, real love.

"You seem happy about them" Duke spoke, noticing my intense stares and satisfied smile

"I am, they deserve it" I replied as we neared the gallery

"They do" He agreed, smiling down at me as I squeezed his hand.

We made it to the gallery within half an hour and entered the crisp white walled building, it's insides holding quiet guests carefully examining framed creativity.

Jaymi tugged Riley along, pointing out her favourites as he seemed to enjoy the museum more than expected. I once again smiled, returning my attention to Duke as we slowly strolled along.

We stopped at a familiar painting and stared at it as I leaned my head on Duke's arm. He twisted his arm around my waist, letting my head fall on the side of his chest as I examined the painting I had grown to love. It was the same one I had fallen for with Jaymi on our adventure.

Hung on the white wall was the thin framed painting of the couple kissing under a street lamp. It's perfection never ceased to amaze me, every stroke creating deep emotion.

"I'll miss this painting when we have to leave" I smiled as I stared at it, resting my head against Dukes cold body

"If we leave" Duke smiled as I looked up at him

I smiled and thought about that reality. Maybe I didn't want to go back, maybe staying here would be the better choice. We could buy a little cottage, like the one I had dreamed about, we could live out our love happily in our own little world.

"Rosie! Hey!" A voice called from behind me

Duke and I quickly turned our heads, Duke's arm never leaving my waist.

Milton Keynes UK
Ingram Content Group UK Ltd.
UKHW021106031224
452078UK00010B/778